Presented to

_____

By

_____

On

_____

For my son, Jacob

Be strong and courageous. Do not be afraid; do not be discouraged,
for the LORD your God will be with you wherever you go.
Joshua 1:9

–J.S.

For mom and dad
–Q.L.

ZONDERKIDZ

God's Little Lambs Bible Stories
Copyright © 2016 by Julie Stiegemeyer
Illustrations © 2016 by Qin Leng

This title is also available as a Zondervan ebook. Visit www.zondervan.com/ebooks.

Requests for information should be addressed to:

Zonderkidz, 3900 *Sparks Dr. SE, Grand Rapids, Michigan 49546*

ISBN 978-0-310-72364-6

Art direction and design: Jody Langley

Printed in China

16 17 18 19 20 21 /LPC/ 22 21 20 19 18 17 16 15 14 13 12 11 10 9 8 7 6 5 4 3 2 1

God's Little Lambs
~ Bible Stories ~

written by Julie Stiegemeyer

illustrated by Qin Leng

ZONDERkidz

Table of Contents

OLD TESTAMENT

NEW TESTAMENT

Old Testament

Who is God?

Genesis 1:1, 17:1; Psalm 90:1–2, 118:1; Isaiah 6:3;
Matthew 3:17; 1 John 4:8

Before anything else was in the world,
before sun or moon,
maple trees or lilac bushes,
before snowflakes or fireflies,
poodles or chickens or fluffy lambs,
and before people,
there was God.

God has always been.
God will always be.

What is God like?
God is powerful.
God is perfect.

God is good.

God is love.

God's love has always been.
God's love will always be.

Before anything else,
God was. And he will
always be there for us.

It Was Good

Genesis 1:1–2:3; Psalm 33:6, 9; Hebrews 11:3

God made everything in the world.
He made tall mountains and tiny grains of sand.
He made sour lemons and sweet juicy pineapple.
He made roaring lions and buzzing bumblebees.
He made smooth seashells and rough tree bark.
God made everything.
He made it all in six days.

On the first day, God made light.
He made day and night.
And God saw that it was good.

On the second day, God made land and water.
He called the land Earth and the water Sea.
And God saw that it was good.

On the third day, God made plants.
He made pine trees, blueberry bushes, sunflowers,
and all sorts of other growing things.
And God saw that it was good.

On the fourth day, God made the sun and moon.
He made the sun to shine during the day,
and the moon to glow through the night.
And God saw that it was good.

On the fifth day, God made fish to swim in the water
and birds to fly in the sky.
He made big floppy fish and small squiggly seahorses.
He made birds with white feathers, black feathers, and
all the colors in between.
And God saw that it was good.

Then, on the sixth day, God made a man and a woman.
He called the man Adam, and the woman he called Eve.
And God saw that it was very good.

On the seventh day, God rested.
That was good too.

God made everything in
the world. God made you
too, and that is very good.

Adam and Eve in the Garden of Eden

Genesis 1:26–31, 2:7–3:24

When God made Adam and Eve, he gave them the
Garden of Eden.

God said, "Here is a beautiful garden for you. You can eat
anything from this garden. But don't eat from one special
tree. If you eat from this tree, you'll die."

Adam and Eve listened to God, and everything was perfect.

Then one day, a snake found Eve in the garden.

"Eve," the snake said. "You should eat this fruit."

"No," Eve said. "God said not to eat from that tree."

"But if you eat from it," the snake said, "you will know everything!"

Eve wasn't sure.

She went to find Adam. "Let's eat some of that fruit," she told him.

So they did.

God found them in the garden.
"Why did you eat from that tree?" God asked them.
"I told you not to."
Adam said, "Eve told me to."
Eve said, "The snake told me to."
"No," God said. "*I* told you not to. You should have listened."

The perfect garden was no longer perfect.
Adam and Eve disobeyed God.
They had to leave the garden.
But God still loved them and promised to
help them.

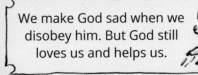

We make God sad when we
disobey him. But God still
loves us and helps us.

A Flood Covers the Earth

Genesis 6:5–8:22

A man named Noah loved and trusted God,
but many people sinned and didn't do what God said.
So God wanted to make things better again.
First, he needed to talk to Noah.
Noah," God said, "I want you to build a big boat called an ark.
I'm going to send a lot of rain to cover the earth.
But you'll be safe in the ark."

Noah listened to God and obeyed.
People pointed at Noah.
"Why are you building a big boat?" they asked.
"We don't live near the water!"
"You're crazy, Noah!"
Noah didn't listen to them. He finished building the boat.

God told Noah to put two of every kind of animal on the boat.
Noah found trumpeting elephants, creeping lizards, and wriggling snakes.
He found leaping monkeys and racing cheetahs.
He found tall-necked giraffes and wooly lambs.
Noah put all of these animals on the boat.
Then Noah and his family got on the boat.
And God shut the door.

Then it rained and rained and rained.
Water covered everything on earth.
Finally, the rain stopped and the water soaked in.

Soon the ark landed on dry ground.
Noah and his family and all of the animals got off the boat.
God made a beautiful rainbow in the sky.

God took care of Noah and his family and kept them safe.
God protected all of the animals.
He promised to never send such a big rain again.

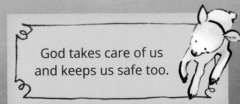

God takes care of us
and keeps us safe too.

The Tower of Babel

Genesis 9–11:9

After the flood, many years passed. Noah's family grew.
They all spoke the same way in the same language.
But they did not listen to God.
They wanted to be greater than God.

One day, the people went to a wide open place.
"Let's build a big tower," they said. "The tower could go as high as heaven.
Then everyone will know how great we are."

So they started building.
Up, up the tower grew, taller and taller.
"Aren't we great?" they said to each other.
"We're even greater than God. We don't need him!"

God saw the tower.
He saw that the people were not listening to him.
He saw that they did not love him.
He saw that they loved only themselves.

So God mixed up their languages.

"Gobbledeegook, blahbaba," it sounded like one said.
"Dublubbaskuk!" another said.
"Blaba?" one asked confused.
"Sniputat?" another asked.
When the people tried to talk, they didn't understand each other.
They were confused.

They stopped building the tower.
It was time for them to learn to love God.

We know that God loves us.
He wants us to love him too.

God Gives Abraham and Sarah a Son

Genesis 17, 21:1–7

God made a promise to a man named Abram.
When Abram was ninety-nine years old, the Lord
came to talk to him.
"Abram," God said. "Walk before me and be perfect.
Then I will give you many children and
grandchildren.
You will no longer be Abram. I will call you
Abraham."
Abraham bowed down and worshipped God.
God had promised to give him a child.
But Abraham and his wife, Sarah, were very old.

A long time went by.
Abraham and Sarah began to wonder if God would
keep his promise.

Finally, God gave them a son.
"Look, Abraham," said Sarah, smiling.
"It's our beautiful baby boy!"
Abraham said, "Let's name him Isaac."
They held Isaac and looked into his eyes.

They knew one thing was true:
God always keeps his promises.

We can trust in God too,
because he always keeps
his promises.

Joseph and His Brothers

Genesis 37, 41–45

Many years after Isaac grew up, his son Jacob had twelve sons.
Of all his sons, Jacob loved Joseph the most.
"Here, Joseph," Jacob said. "I made you a special coat."

But his brothers said, "Why don't we get any good stuff?"
"I'm sick of Joseph!" another said.
"Let's get rid of him!" said a third.

So one day while Joseph was taking care of the sheep,
his brothers planned something bad.
They sold Joseph to a man who took him to a land called Egypt.

Life in Egypt was hard for Joseph.
He worked night and day.
He missed his mother and father.
He missed his brothers even though they had been mean to him.
But he remembered that God was always with him.

Soon the king heard that Joseph could understand dreams.
"Joseph," the king said, "I've been dreaming about fat and skinny cows.
What does this mean?"
Joseph said, "It means that in seven years, there will not be enough food to eat.
We should save plenty of food now so that no one will be hungry later."
"You're very wise," the king said. "You'll be in charge of saving the food."

Joseph filled big barns with food so the people in Egypt could eat.
But people in other places didn't have enough, including Joseph's brothers.

Joseph's brothers came to Egypt.
"Could we have some food? We're hungry!
We're so sorry we sent you away," they said.
Joseph bowed his head.
His brothers had hurt him, but God had helped.

Joseph said, "I forgive you for what you did.
God took something bad and made it good."
Joseph gave them food to eat and showed
them love and forgiveness.

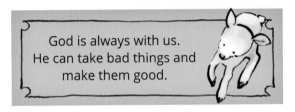

God is always with us.
He can take bad things and
make them good.

God Saves Baby Moses

Exodus 1:1–2:10

Joseph's family stayed in Egypt. His family grew and grew.
They were God's people.
Years passed.
The new king in Egypt did not like God's people.
"Let's get them," the king said. "Go get rid of all the baby boys!"

One of those baby boys was Moses.
His mother was worried.
She didn't want anything bad to happen to Moses.
She wanted to hide Moses from the king.

Moses' mother called her daughter Miriam.
"Help me hide your little brother.
We'll put him in a basket to keep him safe."
They went down to the river.
They placed the basket in the water, and Moses floated away.
Miriam stood nearby and watched.

43

Then a princess saw the basket.
When she opened the basket, she saw Moses.
"Look, a baby!" she said. He was crying.
She wanted to take Moses home with her.
"He needs someone to care for him," she said.

Miriam was watching. She stepped forward.
"Shall I get someone who can help you?" she asked.
"Yes," the princess said.
So Miriam ran to get her mother.
Her mother cared for Moses in the palace.
And Moses grew up protected by God.
God had special plans for Moses.

God has special plans for you too.

God Talks to Moses

Exodus 3

One day, after Moses grew up,
he was out in the fields taking care of his sheep.
He looked over and saw a bush.
The bush was on fire!
But it did not burn up.

Then Moses heard someone say his name.
"Moses! Moses!" the voice said.
"Here I am," Moses said.

The voice said, "Moses, I am God."
Moses was afraid and covered his face.

"You will take my people out of Egypt into a new land," God said. "Tell the king to let my people go."

Moses said, "Lord, what if the king doesn't believe you've sent me? What if he won't let your people go?"

God said, "Take your stick. Throw it on the ground." Moses did it. The stick turned into a snake!

"Now, pick it up," God said.

Moses reached down and picked it up.

It became a stick again!

God said, "Show this to the king. Then he will believe you."

Moses did what God told him.

Moses was afraid, but God helped Moses do amazing things.

We may also be afraid,
but God will help us.
He always does.

God's People and the Red Sea

Exodus 14

Moses led God's people out of Egypt.
But the king's soldiers went after them.
Soon God's people came to the Red Sea.
The sea was in front of them.
The soldiers were behind them.
They could not go forward.
They could not go backward.
They were stuck!

Moses said to the people:
"Don't be afraid! The Lord will fight for you."

God told Moses to hold out his stick.
When Moses did this, God pushed the sea back by a strong wind.
God blew back the water all night long.
Soon there was a path.
The people walked through the sea on dry ground.
A wall of water stood to the right and to the left.

God's people walked right through the sea.
God saved his people!
When they got to the other side of the sea,
they danced and praised God.
"The Lord is my help and my strength," they sang.
"He is my God, and we will praise him!"

We remember God's
amazing work,
and we thank him too.

God Gives His People Rules

Exodus 19–20

God took care of his people.
He took them away from Egypt and away from the bad king.
Now God's people were walking to a new land.
It was time for them to learn God's rules.

God came to Moses, "Tell the people to get ready.
I am coming to Mount Sinai to talk to you."

When God came down, there was thunder and lightning.
A thick cloud covered the mountain.
A trumpet blasted.
The people trembled in fear.
"Moses," the Lord said, "come up to the mountain."
So up, up, up Moses climbed.

At the top of the mountain, God talked to Moses:
"I am the Lord your God," he said.
"I brought you out of the land of Egypt.
Don't have any other gods.
Don't say my name in a bad way.
Have a day of rest and worship me.
Obey your mother and father.
Don't hurt anyone.
Moms and dads should love each other.
Don't take what doesn't belong to you.
Don't say anything that will hurt someone.
Always tell the truth.
Be happy with what I give you."

Moses came down from the mountain.
He told the people God's rules.
The people trembled in fear.
Moses said, "Do not be afraid. God's rules are good for us.
Let's follow them."

God had taken care of his people.
Now he wanted them to do what was right.

We are God's people too, and God wants us to do the right thing.

Joshua and the Big Battle

Joshua 6

Joshua became the leader of God's people.
God told Joshua to go into a new land.
"Be strong," God said. "I will go with you."
Joshua told the people, "Let's go!"
So they went into the new land.

"Here is a big city," God told Joshua.
"I want you to be in charge of it.
But first, the wall around the city needs to be
knocked down."

God's people were confused.
How could they knock down such a big wall?
"Be strong," God told Joshua. "I will go with you."

"Walk around that big wall for six days," God said.
"Take your trumpets, but do not blow them. Not yet.
On the seventh day," God said, "shout and blow your
trumpets!
Be strong," God told them. "I will go with you."

For six days, God's people walked around that big wall.
They didn't shout.
They didn't blow their trumpets.

On the seventh day, they walked around the big wall again.
This time, they shouted!
They blew their trumpets!
And what did God do?
God made that wall fall down flat! *Crash!*
God helped Joshua be strong. He helped the people be strong.

God helps us be strong too.

David and Goliath

1 Samuel 17

A mighty army came to fight God's people.
In this army was a soldier named Goliath.
Goliath scared everyone.
He was strong.
He was mighty.
He was powerful.
God's people had to fight him,
but even the strongest soldiers were afraid.

A young shepherd boy named David heard about Goliath.
David stepped up. "I will fight him!" he said.
"No," God's people said.
"You are not big enough to fight him.
Goliath is strong!
Goliath is mighty!
Goliath is powerful!"

But David said, "See my sling?
With it, the Lord has helped me kill lions and bears that try
to hurt my lambs.
The Lord will help me kill Goliath too."

So David found five smooth stones from the river.
He took his sling and shot those stones right at Goliath.
And the Lord helped David.
The Lord was stronger.
The Lord was mightier.
The Lord was even more powerful.
The Lord helped David knock Goliath to the ground.

Sometimes we may feel small, but God is strong and mighty and powerful.

David Sings Before the Lord

1 Samuel 17, Psalm 23

When David was a boy, he took care of his father's sheep. He made sure the sheep got food.

He protected the little lambs from lions and bears.
He killed the mighty soldier Goliath.

David grew up and became a mighty king.
David also sang and played music before the Lord.
He wrote many songs.

Once, he sang:
"The Lord is my shepherd.
He makes me lie down in green pastures.
He leads me beside still waters.
He restores my soul.

"God guides my footsteps.
He is always with me.
And one day he will take me to heaven with him."

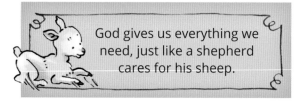

God gives us everything we need, just like a shepherd cares for his sheep.

Three Men in the Fiery Furnace

Daniel 3

One time a king built a golden statue.
He said, "Everyone must kneel down to worship
my statue."

Three men named Shadrach, Meshach, and
Abednego did not kneel down.
They did not do what the king said.

The king called Shadrach, Meshach, and
Abednego before him.
He said, "Is it true that you will not worship my
golden statue?"
"No, we won't," they said. "We will only worship God,
the one true God."
That made the king angry.

73

The king said, "I will throw you in a blazing hot furnace!"
They said, "We will only worship the one true God."
The king roared, "I will make my furnace even hotter!"
But they said, "We will only worship the one true God."
They trusted that the Lord would protect them.

The king threw the three men into the furnace.
It was blazing hot.
But when the king looked, he couldn't believe his eyes!
Shadrach, Meshach, and Abednego were walking around
in the furnace.
The king saw an angel in the fire too.

"Come out of the furnace," the king said.
Shadrach, Meshach, and Abednego came out.
The fire hadn't hurt them.
Their clothes didn't even smell like smoke.

The king said, "Praise be to the one true God.
God sent his angel to save you!"

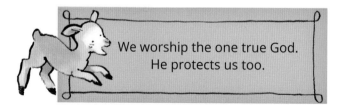

We worship the one true God.
He protects us too.

Daniel in the Lions' Den

Daniel 6

A man named Daniel believed in God.
He trusted that God would care for him.
Daniel kneeled down and prayed to God three times every day.

Daniel was also a good helper to King Darius.
Some of his other helpers wanted to get rid of Daniel, so
they tricked the king.
"O, king," they said. "You should make a rule that everyone
should pray only to you."
The king liked this idea.
"Now it is the law", he said.

The next day, Daniel prayed to God like he always did.
The bad men hid nearby and watched him.

Then they ran to the king.
"O, King," they said. "Someone broke your rules.
He was praying, but not to you.
Now you have to throw him into the den of lions!"

"Who did this?" the king asked.

"Daniel," they said.

The king was sad because he liked Daniel.

"May your God rescue you!" the king said to Daniel.

The men came and threw Daniel into the lions' den.

But Daniel kept praying.

The next morning, the king called to Daniel, "Has your God saved you?"

"Yes," Daniel said. "My God sent his angel. The lions have not hurt me."

The king took Daniel out of the lions' den.

The king got rid of his old rule and made a new one:

"Everyone must worship the one true God," the king said.

"For he is the living God!

He has delivered Daniel from the lions!"

We pray to God,
just like Daniel.

79

Jonah and the Big Fish

Jonah 1–2

God had a special job for a man named Jonah.
"Jonah," God told him. "Go to a place called Nineveh.
Tell them about me, and tell them to obey my laws."
But Jonah didn't want to go.
So he ran away.

Jonah found a big boat that would sail far away.
But God sent a big wind to the boat.
The boat started rocking.
The waves got higher and higher.
The people on the boat got scared.
They thought the boat might break apart.

"Jonah," they said. "Ask God to save us from this storm!"
Jonah knew God sent the storm.
"Pick me up and throw me into the water," Jonah said.
"Then the wind will stop."
The people didn't want to, but they threw Jonah out of the boat.
The raging water grew calm.

Jonah was alone in the water until a big fish came along.
That big fish swallowed Jonah up!

Jonah was inside the belly of the fish for three days and nights.
"O, Lord," Jonah said. "Hear my voice. Please save me."
Then God told the fish to get rid of Jonah.
So the fish swam up to the shore and spit Jonah out.

After that, Jonah bowed down.
"Thank you, God, for saving me.
I will do what you asked me to do.
I will go to the people of Nineveh and tell them about you."
The people listened to Jonah and believed in God.

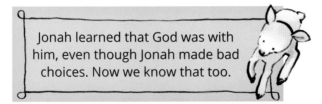

Jonah learned that God was with him, even though Jonah made bad choices. Now we know that too.

New
Testament

God's Greatest Gift

Luke 1:26–38, 2:1–7

A young woman named Mary lived in a village called Nazareth.
She would soon marry a man named Joseph.
But a surprising thing happened first.

One day, an angel from heaven named Gabriel visited Mary
at her house.
"Don't be afraid," Gabriel said. "I have good news for you!"
Mary was surprised! God sent an angel to talk to her.

"Mary," the angel said, "soon, Jesus, the Son of God,
will come into the world.
"You are going to be his mother."

Mary was amazed. "How can this be?" she asked.
Then she remembered that God can do anything.
Mary said, "I serve the Lord. I am ready to do what God
wants me to do."

The time came for Jesus to be born.
But Mary and Joseph had to travel a long way from home.
They came to a town called Bethlehem, but no one had room for them.
So Mary and Joseph stayed in a stable with the donkeys, sheep, and lambs.

That night, Mary gave birth to Jesus.
She didn't have a soft bed where she could lay her baby.
She didn't have a crib with comfy blankets.
All she had for Jesus was a manger, the place where animals ate their food.
This was part of God's plan.
And Mary knew Jesus would be God's greatest gift.

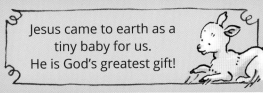

Jesus came to earth as a
tiny baby for us.
He is God's greatest gift!

Visitors Come to See Jesus

Matthew 2:1–12; Luke 2:8–20

One night, some shepherds were out in the fields caring for
their sheep.
Suddenly, an angel appeared.
"Do not be afraid," the angel said.
"I bring you good news of great joy!
Today, a Savior has been born for you.
You will see a baby wrapped in cloths and lying in a manger."

The shepherds were amazed.
"Let's go to Bethlehem!" they said to each other.
So they hurried off.
They found Mary and Joseph and the baby Jesus.
After they had seen Jesus, they told everyone about him.

Later, some wise men came to see Jesus.
These men were from a faraway country.
They traveled by a star's light.
The star went ahead of them until it stopped
over the place where Jesus was.
The wise men were so happy to see the child
with his mother.
They bowed down and worshipped Jesus.
Then they opened their gifts of gold, incense,
and myrrh.

The shepherds and wise men
knew Jesus was special.
We know it too.

The Boy Jesus in the Temple

Luke 2:41–52

Jesus grew up in Nazareth.
When he was twelve years old, he went with his family to visit Jerusalem.
They went to worship God in his house, the temple.

Soon it was time to go home.
The big family started the long trip back home.
After many hours, Mary and Joseph could not find Jesus.
"Is Jesus with you?" Mary asked his aunts and uncles.
"No," they said.
"Is Jesus with you?" Joseph asked the other kids.
"No," they said.
Where was he?

Mary and Joseph went back to the city.
They looked everywhere.
Where could Jesus be?

Finally, they found him in God's house.
Jesus was talking to the important leaders.
Jesus was just a boy, but he was teaching them.

Mary and Joseph were upset.
"Jesus," they said. "We couldn't find you!
Why weren't you with us?"
But Jesus said, "Why were you worried?
Didn't you know I'd be in my Father's house?"

Jesus was God's Son.
Soon he would be teaching people all the time.
But it was time to go back home with Mary and Joseph.
Jesus obeyed them and continued to grow strong and wise.

God gives us parents to care for us. It's important to do the things our parents ask, just like Jesus did.

John Baptizes Jesus

Matthew 3:1–17; John 1:29–34

Jesus became a man.
He worked with Joseph as a carpenter.
They made things out of wood.
Soon the time came for Jesus to do what God sent him to do.

John, Jesus' cousin, loved God.
John told people about God.
He baptized people in the Jordan River.
One day, Jesus came to John at the river.
"Baptize me," Jesus said.

John said, "No, Jesus, I should be baptized by you!"
Jesus replied, "It is right to do this."

So John baptized Jesus.
Then the sky opened.
God's voice spoke from the sky, "This is my Son."
Then a dove came down on Jesus.
The dove was a sign of God's blessing.
Jesus was here to do special work,
to love and help people.
Now everyone else knew it too.

We know that Jesus' special work of loving and helping was for us too.

Jesus Helps Peter Catch Fish

Luke 5:1–11

Peter, one of Jesus' friends, was fishing.
Jesus asked him, "Can I use your boat?"
Peter said yes.

Jesus got in the boat.
He stood up and talked to the people gathered on the shore.
Jesus told the people about God.
He was doing the special work God wanted him to do.

Then Jesus said to Peter, "Go out into the deep water to catch some fish."
Peter said, "Lord, I have been out fishing all night.
I didn't catch a single fish."
But Peter threw nets into the water anyway.

Then Jesus made an amazing
thing happen.
Peter pulled up his nets.
They were full of wiggling fish—
so many fish that Peter could
barely lift the nets!

Peter could hardly believe it!
Jesus made a miracle happen.

We know that Jesus also does wonderful things for us.

Jesus Makes a Storm Go Away

Mark 4:35–41

Jesus was with his friends on a boat going to the
other side of a lake.
Jesus had been teaching all day. He was tired.
The gentle rocking of the boat lulled him to sleep.
Suddenly, a big storm came.
Wind howled!
Water splashed!
Waves crashed!
The boat rocked back and forth.

Jesus' friends shook with fear.
"Our boat might sink!" they shouted.
"Jesus!" they cried. "Don't you care about us?
We might die. Help us!"
But Jesus was still sleeping.

Jesus woke up.
He spoke to the wind.
"Hush!"
He spoke to the water.
"Be still!"

The wind stopped howling.
The water stopped splashing.
The waves stopped crashing.
Everything was quiet.

Then Jesus said to his friends,
"Why were you afraid? I am here with you."

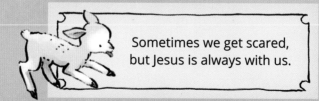

Sometimes we get scared,
but Jesus is always with us.

Jesus Helps

Luke 17:11–19

Every day Jesus was doing God's work.
He told people about God.
He made sick people well.

He made blind people see.

He made deaf people hear.

One day ten sick men shouted to Jesus,
"Please help us. We know you can help."
Their skin had painful sores.
They couldn't be with other people because they might
get them sick too.

Jesus made an amazing thing happen.
The men were healed!
Their skin was clean and smooth again.
They shouted and jumped for joy.
Jesus took their sickness away.
He said, "Go and show everyone that you are now well."
The men ran to tell everyone their great news.

One man turned and ran back to Jesus.
"Thank you for healing me," he said.
"Thank you for making me well again."

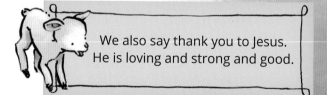

We also say thank you to Jesus.
He is loving and strong and good.

Jesus Gives Food to Many

John 6:1–13

One morning, Jesus walked up a big hill to teach a
crowd of people.
They loved listening to Jesus talk about God.

Soon it was lunchtime, and everyone got hungry.
With so many people, they would need a lot of
food.
Jesus' friends worried.
"Where will we find enough food?" they asked.

A boy walked up to Jesus' friends.
"Here," he said. "I have bread and fish.
I will share this with everyone."
But the boy only had a small lunch.

Jesus prayed before they ate.

"Thank you, God, for this food," he said.

His friends passed out basket after basket of bread and fish.

The bread and fish never ran out.

Everyone ate and ate.

There was enough for everyone!

Jesus did a miracle.

Jesus showed the people that God can do anything.

Before we eat our food, we thank God. He always gives us what we need.

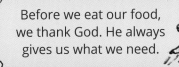

Jesus Welcomes the Children

Mark 10:13–16

One day while Jesus was teaching, some people
brought their children to him.
"Jesus," they said. "Will you bless my child?"
But Jesus' helpers didn't want the kids to bother Jesus.
"Go away," they said, pushing the people back.
"Leave Jesus alone."

"No," Jesus said. "Let the children come to me."
He opened his arms wide.
The children ran to him.

Jesus laughed and smiled.
He wrapped his arms around the children.
He blessed them.

Jesus loves everyone, big and small.
He loves moms, dads, grandmas,
and grandpas. And he really loves
children—including you!

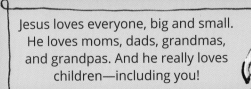

A Woman Washes Jesus' Feet

Luke 7:36–50

One night, Jesus went to Simon's house for dinner.
Jesus and his friends were eating when a woman
walked in.
She poured perfume on Jesus' head.
She cried tears to wash Jesus' feet.
She dried his feet with her long hair.
She was showing her love for Jesus.

Jesus' friends didn't like this woman. They thought
she was bad.
Simon frowned at her. "Leave Jesus alone," he said.

But Jesus turned to Simon.

"When I came to your house, did you wash my feet, Simon?"

"No," he said.

"Did you put perfume on my head?"

Simon shook his head. He was embarrassed.

He had not done anything special for Jesus.

But this woman had.

"She has shown great love," Jesus said.

Then he smiled at the woman.

"God forgives your sins. Go in peace and do good."

Jesus forgives our
sins too.
Thank you, Jesus!

Jesus Visits Zacchaeus

Luke 19:1–9

Zacchaeus was a rich man from Jericho.
His job was a tax collector. But he did something bad.
He took money that didn't belong to him.

Jesus came to visit Jericho. A big crowd gathered
around Jesus.
Zacchaeus wanted to see him too.
He was a short man, so he couldn't see over the other
people.
He got on his tiptoes.
He still couldn't see.
He jumped up and up.
But he still couldn't see.

Zacchaeus had an idea. A sycamore tree was close by.
He could climb it!
So he climbed up, up, high above the people.
Now he could see!
Then Jesus looked up at Zacchaeus.

"Zacchaeus," Jesus said. "Come down from the tree.
I want to have dinner with you."
Zacchaeus smiled. Jesus wanted to be with him.

Jesus loved Zacchaeus.
Zacchaeus felt so happy inside.
He wanted to make Jesus happy too.
He said, "Lord, I'm sorry for everything I've done wrong.
I'll fix it and give half of my money to poor people."
Jesus smiled and said,
"Today you are a new man, Zacchaeus."

Jesus came to help everybody—
good and bad.
He came to help us too.

Jesus Rides into Town

John 12:12–19

Jesus and his friends were on their way to Jerusalem.
When they were close to the city, Jesus said,
"Go into the city ahead of me.
You will find a donkey just for me."
His friends found the donkey and brought it to Jesus.
Jesus rode the donkey into the city.
The donkey's hooves *clip-clopped* on the road.

131

The people saw Jesus and cheered.
It was a parade!
Moms and dads and children came to see Jesus.
They put their coats on the ground to make a
special path.
"Hosanna!" they cheered.
They put leafy palm branches on the ground.
"Hosanna!" they cried.

The people loved Jesus, their king.
"Hosanna!" they said. "Blessed is he who
comes in the name of the Lord."

Jesus is our King.
We cheer for him.

Jesus Gives a Special Meal and Prays

Luke 22:7–20, 39–44

Jesus and his twelve best friends visited Jerusalem for a few days.
They shared a special meal for the Passover holiday.
Jesus took some bread and broke it in pieces.
He said, "Take this and eat. This is my body, given for you."

Then Jesus took wine and said,
"Take this and drink. This is my blood shed for you."
Jesus' friends ate and drank with him.

After their special meal, Jesus went out to a
garden to pray.
Peter, James, and John came along.
Jesus asked them to pray with him.
He said, "Don't fall asleep, but pray."

Jesus talked to his heavenly Father.
He knew that the time was coming for him to
do his most important work.
He knew that it would be hard.
But he also knew that his Father loved him.
So he asked for help.
"Father," he prayed, "I will do what you want."

God wants us to talk to him
just like Jesus did.

Jesus Dies for Us

Matthew 26:36–56; 27:27–56

Not everyone believed that Jesus was the Son of God.
So some people tried to get rid of him.

In the garden, while Jesus was praying,
some soldiers suddenly arrived.
They roughly pulled Jesus to his feet.
"Come with us," they shouted.

They took him before the governor.
The crowds wanted Jesus to die.
"Kill him! Kill him!" they yelled.
They wanted Jesus to die on a cross.

The soldiers hurt Jesus.
They beat him up.
Then they made Jesus carry a big cross outside the city.
The people shouted at Jesus.

Then they nailed Jesus to the cross.
It really hurt.

Jesus looked down from the cross.
He saw his mother, Mary, and his friend John.
They were crying.

Then Jesus looked down on the people who wanted him to die.
Even though they hurt him, he still loved them.
He prayed, "Father, forgive them."

With one last breath, Jesus died.
Jesus gave up his life so all those people would know
about God's love.

Jesus died because he
wanted to take away our sins.
He died because he loves us.

Jesus Comes Back to Life

Mark 16:1–10 ; Luke 23:50–56; 24:1–8

After Jesus died, his friends took his body down from the cross.
A man named Joseph of Arimathea helped.
He wrapped Jesus' body in cloth.
He gently laid Jesus' body in a quiet tomb.
Soldiers rolled a large stone in front of the tomb.
Jesus' body lay there for three days.

On the third day, some women brought spices to put on
Jesus' body.
Mary Magdalene was one of them.

The women wondered how they would move the large stone.
But when they arrived, they saw the stone was moved away and
the tomb was open.
They looked inside. Jesus' body was gone.
"Where is he?" they said. "Where could he be?"

Suddenly, an angel appeared.
The angel's clothing was bright as lightning and white as snow.
"Jesus is not here. He is risen!" the angel said.
The women could hardly believe it. Jesus was alive?

Then a man went to Mary Magdalene.
She thought it was the gardener.
She asked, "Sir, do you know where Jesus' body is?"
The man simply said, "Mary."

Mary knew that voice.
It was not the gardener.
It was Jesus!
He was alive!

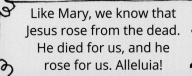

Like Mary, we know that Jesus rose from the dead. He died for us, and he rose for us. Alleluia!

Jesus Goes up to Heaven

Matthew 28:16–20; Luke 24:36–53

After Jesus rose from the dead, he spent time with his friends.
Jesus said to them, "Go! Tell everyone about God.
Teach and baptize people from every land and nation."

Forty days later, Jesus had to go back to heaven.
Before he left, he raised his hands and blessed his friends.
"Remember, I will be with you always," Jesus told them.

147

Jesus' friends watched as Jesus went up to heaven.
A cloud took Jesus out of their sight.
Then they went back to Jerusalem with great joy.
They could not stop praising God in the temple.
Jesus' friends thanked God for all that he had done for them.
They started sharing this good news with others.

We can share the good news of God's love!

A Crippled Man Walks

Acts 3

Jesus' friends told everyone they met about Jesus.
One day, two of his friends, Peter and John, were going to pray.
A man who could not walk sat near the road.
When Peter and John walked by, the man said,
"Please, can you give me some money?
I need to buy something to eat."

Peter said, "We do not have silver or gold.
We can give you something even better."
Then Peter said, "In the name of Jesus Christ, walk!"
He reached out his hand to help the man stand up.

Suddenly, the man's ankles became strong.
His knees became strong.

His legs became strong.

He walked.

He stood up.
He jumped.

He praised God!

All the people were surprised!
Peter healed the man through Jesus' name.
Then Peter told the people all about Jesus.

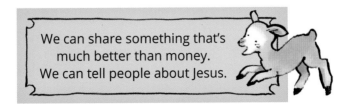

We can share something that's
much better than money.
We can tell people about Jesus.

Paul Tells about Jesus

Acts 27:13–38

One of Jesus' followers was a man named Paul.
Paul traveled many places to tell others about God.
He walked through the dusty roads.

He rode on a donkey that *clip-clopped* along
pathways.
He sailed in a boat across the rocking waves.
Everywhere Paul went, he told people about
Jesus and God's love.

Once when Paul was sailing across the sea, a big storm came.
Clouds gathered.
Wind blew.
Rain poured.

"Oh no!" the people cried.
"Our boat might hit the rocks and break apart!
What will we do?" they asked.

Paul knew what to do.
He kneeled down.
He talked to God.
He asked God to save them.
The rain splashed on Paul's face as the boat tipped and swayed.
He kept praying.

After the long night, the sun rose.
Soon the boat landed safely on the shore.
God had kept them safe.

Now Paul could share the good news about Jesus' love.
Paul and Jesus' other friends told everyone they met about Jesus.
They told about his great love.
They shared his love all over the world.

God's great love is for everyone in every place. What good news!